READING CHAMPION

The Prince and the Pea

by Katie Dale and Ryan Wheatcroft

W

Chapter 1

Once upon a time there lived a lonely prince called Rupert. Every day, Rupert watched the village children playing. He longed to join in, but the Queen wouldn't let him. The village children were rough and tough. She was worried Rupert would get hurt.

"I know," the Queen thought. "Rupert needs a royal playmate! A nice princess to play games with." But how could she find the right princess?

The Queen read books to discover how other princes had found princesses. Some princes had rescued their princesses from tall towers, witches or dragons.

"Far too dangerous!" the Queen cried.

Another prince had held a ball, but ended up dancing with a servant girl in disguise!

"How awful!" the Queen gasped.

But how could you tell if someone was truly a princess? Suddenly, the Queen found the answer.

Chapter 2

"Rupert," the Queen cried, bursting through the door one morning. "Meet Princess Emilia!" Rupert's eyes lit up. He was finally allowed to have a playmate! He couldn't wait to play with Emilia.

But Emilia was no fun at all. All she wanted to do was play the violin – very loudly and very badly. Rupert covered his ears. He couldn't wait for Emilia to go home.

To Rupert's horror, the Queen invited Emilia to sleep over! She'd even made her a special bed, piled high with forty mattresses. Then, when Emilia went to brush her teeth, Rupert saw the Queen put a pea under the mattresses in Emilia's bed.

"What are you doing?" Rupert asked.

"I have a clever plan," the Queen smiled. "If Emilia can feel this pea through all these mattresses, it will prove that she is a **real** princess!"

7

"Why do you need to know that?" Rupert asked, frowning.

"Because only a real princess is good enough to be your regular playmate, my darling," the Queen said, hugging him. "Then you won't be lonely any more."

Rupert was worried. He'd rather be lonely than play with awful Emilia ever again! Then Rupert had a clever plan of his own. When the Queen wasn't looking, he removed the pea.

"Good morning, Emilia," said the Queen
the next morning. "Did you sleep well?"

"Very well," Emilia said. "That was the most
comfortable bed I've ever slept in!"

The Queen frowned. Rupert grinned. His plan
had worked.

Chapter 3

But the Queen didn't give up. She invited

more and more princesses to stay.

Each one was more boring than the last.

One girl spent all day gazing at the palace jewels.

One talked non-stop.

Another didn't

talk at all!

Every day the Queen placed a pea underneath

the towering mattresses. And every evening

Rupert removed it before bedtime.

I can't believe it," the Queen sighed. "None

of these girls are real princesses."

Rupert hid his grin.

"Oh well," the Queen said. "Princess Clarabel is

coming tonight. Maybe she'll be the one."

But the hours ticked by and there was no

sign of Princess Clarabel. A storm raged outside.

"Maybe she's not coming?" Rupert said, hopefully.

He'd had enough boring princesses to last a lifetime.

"Nonsense. She's probably just been delayed

by this horrible storm," the Queen replied,

gazing out of the window.

Finally, there was a knock at the door. A girl stood dripping on the doorstep.

"Hi," she said. "I'm – "

"Why, you must be Clarabel!" the Queen cried, hugging her. "We've been expecting you. Let's get you some dry clothes, and some dinner! What would you like? Smoked salmon? Roast venison?"

"Have you got any fish fingers?" Clarabel asked.

The Queen's eyes widened. "I didn't even know fish had fingers. How exotic!"

Rupert had never tried fish fingers before. They were delicious.

"Shall we listen to some music now?" the Queen suggested.

"I could play for you?" Clarabel offered.

"Yes please," the Queen cried. "How delightful!"

Rupert sighed. Not more horrible screechy violin music ...

But it wasn't. Clarabel played the drums.

"That was amazing!" Rupert cried. "Can you

teach me?"

"Not now, it's bedtime," the Queen said, quickly.

Chapter 4

Rupert couldn't sleep. Clarabel was the best playmate yet, he hoped she'd be able to stay. But what if she didn't feel the pea? It was very small, after all. Maybe he should tell her about it? He crept out of his bedroom on to the landing. Then, suddenly, something hit his neck.

It was a pea!

"Ow!" Rupert cried.

"Someone put a pea in my bed," Clarabel said, standing on the landing holding a pea-shooter. "So I thought I'd return it."

Rupert felt his cheeks grow warm. "It wasn't me!"

Clarabel grinned. "Doesn't matter, I can't sleep anyway. Come on, I've found a much better use for all those mattresses."

Clarabel had heaped mattresses all round her room.

"Whee!" she cried, jumping from one pile to another. "They're like trampolines."

"What's a trampoline?" Rupert asked.

Clarabel just laughed. "Bet you can't jump as high as me."

Rupert grinned and bounced after her.

It was great fun. He even tried somersaults!

Have you ever been sledging?" asked Clarabel.

Rupert shook his head. "Mother doesn't let me go outside if it snows. She's afraid I'll get hurt."

"Nonsense. Let's go now!" Clarabel cried.

"But it isn't snowing," Rupert frowned.

"Doesn't matter. We don't even have to go outside," Clarabel laughed. She grabbed a mattress and headed for the grand staircase.

"**Woo-hoo!**" Rupert cried, as they slid down the stairs on a mattress.

"This is the best night **ever**!"

"Yes it is," Clarabel grinned. "But now the sun's coming up. Back to bed! **QUICK!**"

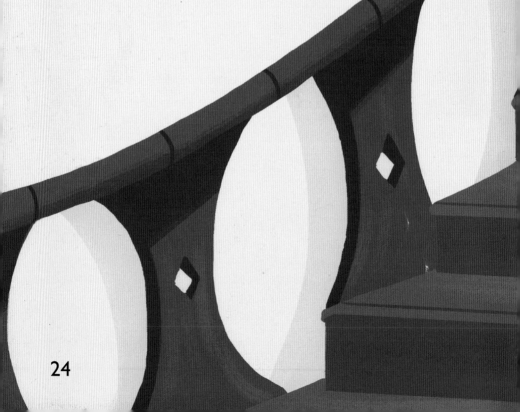

Chapter 5

Just as Rupert and Clarabel had piled up

the mattresses again, the Queen walked in.

"Good morning," she said. "Did you sleep well?"

"Actually, I haven't slept at all," Clarabel

confessed.

"How wonderful!" the Queen exclaimed.

"You must come and play again,

Princess Clarabel."

"Hurray!" Rupert cheered, but Clarabel laughed.

"I'd love to come round to play with the Prince,"
Clarabel said. "But my name's not Princess
Clarabel, it's Evelyn. I live in the village."
Rupert gasped. The Queen was astonished.

"Can Evelyn still visit, Mum?" Rupert asked, hopefully.

The Queen hesitated. But then she looked at Rupert's face. She'd never seen him so happy.

"Yes," she smiled.

"Hurray!" Rupert cheered and suddenly all the Queen's worries disappeared.

Her clever idea hadn't worked out as she'd planned. But, whether Evelyn was a princess or not, she made Rupert happy – and that was all that mattered.

Things to think about

1. Why won't the Queen allow Rupert to play outside with the other children?
2. How does Rupert feel when his mother invites the various Princesses to play with him?
3. What idea does the Queen have for finding a real princess playmate? Where did she get the idea from?
4. What are the similarities and differences with this story and the original fairy tale, *The Princess and the Pea*?

Write it yourself

One of the themes in this story is not following expectations. Now try to write your own story with a similar theme.

Plan your story before you begin to write it.

Start off with a story map:

• a beginning to introduce the characters and where and when your story is set (the setting);

• a problem that the main characters will need to fix in the story;

• an ending where the problems are resolved.

Get writing! Think about a fairy tale or traditional story you know and how you might write a new version of it to convey your idea.

Notes for parents and carers

Independent reading
The aim of independent reading is to read this book with ease. This series is designed to provide an opportunity for your child to read for pleasure and enjoyment. These notes are written for you to help your child make the most of this book.

About the book
In this twist on the classic fairy tale, the young prince is desperate to find a playmate. His mother, the Queen, only wants him to play with a suitable princess and devises a test to find one. But the prince and his mother soon find out that true friendship is more precious than being a real princess.

Before reading
Ask your child why they have selected this book. Look at the title and blurb together. What do they think it will be about? Do they think they will like it?

During reading
Encourage your child to read independently. If they get stuck on a longer word, remind them that they can find syllable chunks that can be sounded out from left to right. They can also read on in the sentence and think about what would make sense.

After reading
Support comprehension by talking about the story. What happened? Then help your child think about the messages in the book that go beyond the story, using the questions on the page opposite. Give your child a chance to respond to the story, asking:
Did you enjoy the story and why? Who was your favourite character?
What was your favourite part? What did you expect to happen at the end?

Franklin Watts
First published in Great Britain in 2018
by The Watts Publishing Group

Series Editors: Jackie Hamley and Melanie Palmer
Series Advisors: Dr Sue Bodman and Glen Franklin
Series Designer: Peter Scoulding

A CIP catalogue record for this book is
available from the British Library.

ISBN 978 1 4451 6338 3 (hbk)
ISBN 978 1 4451 6340 6 (pbk)
ISBN 978 1 4451 6339 0 (library ebook)

Printed in China

Franklin Watts
An imprint of
Hachette Children's Group
Part of The Watts Publishing Group
Carmelite House
50 Victoria Embankment
London EC4Y 0DZ

An Hachette UK Company
www.hachette.co.uk

www.franklinwatts.co.uk